Contents

Chapter 1
Life Force

Japan, Year 1580

Pain rages across my chest like fire and I collapse onto the wooden floor of the temple.

An old man with a wrinkled face, pale eyes and a long grey beard stands over me. He is the Grandmaster of my ninja clan. And he's just given me the Death Touch.

"The Death Touch isn't about power," the Grandmaster explains to the other ninja students who stand around my shaking body. "As you saw, I hardly even hit Taka."

A girl with long black hair drops to her knees beside me. She is my best friend, Cho, and her dark brown eyes are full of concern.

"What have you done to him?" Cho asks as I fight for breath.

"I've blocked his *chi*," the Grandmaster replies.

Among the students is Renzo, a boy of 16, with a shaved head and large muscles. He frowns in confusion. The Grandmaster is blind, but he senses the frown and turns to Renzo.

"The student who asks a question is a fool for a minute. The student who does not ask stays a fool forever," the Grandmaster says.

The rest of the class turn to stare at Renzo too and his face burns red with shame. All the while, I twist in agony on the floor.

After an embarrassed pause, Renzo asks, "What's ... *chi*?"

"It is your life force," the Grandmaster replies with a smile. "It's vital to your existence. You can live for three months without food. You can live for three days without water. You can live for three minutes without air. But you can't live for *one second* without *chi*."

The Grandmaster holds up one bony finger to stress the single second. Then, with the same finger, he traces twelve lines across Renzo's body. "*Chi* flows through invisible energy lines in your body," he explains. "A ninja can use the Death Touch at certain points along these lines. By doing this he can block an opponent's energy. He can destroy their life force. He can even inject bad *chi* into them."

As the Death Touch squeezes the life out of me, the Grandmaster's voice becomes distant in my ears. It's as if he's speaking from the back of a cave. The pain spreads to my arms and legs and I can no longer move.

Cho sees the terror in my eyes. "I think Taka's had enough – " she begins.

Renzo interrupts her. "Is Taka dying?"

"If I don't unblock his *chi*, yes he will die," the Grandmaster replies.

Renzo looks down at me and grins. "Oh dear, that would be a pity," he says. It's obvious he's not upset by the idea at all.

I start to panic. I'm 14 years old, too young to die. My chest now feels as if it's being crushed by a huge rock and I can't breathe.

But the Grandmaster doesn't try to save me.

He just goes on with his lesson. "If you're an expert and know which points on the human body to strike, it's very easy to kill someone with the Death Touch," he explains. "The real skill is *not* killing the person."

"So when do *we* learn the Death Touch?" Renzo asks. He flexes his fingers, keen to begin.

The Grandmaster gives Renzo a stern look. "You must learn to walk before you can run," he replies. "First, I'll teach you the points that will stop your enemy's sword arm. But that will be tomorrow's lesson."

The Grandmaster reaches for his wooden staff and hobbles away.

"Grandmaster!" Cho calls. "What about Taka?"

The Grandmaster stops and turns back with a surprised look on his face. "Sorry, I almost forgot. Old age must be catching up on me," he explains. "Help Taka to stand."

Cho and two other students pick me up. I hang like a broken puppet in their arms.

The Grandmaster presses three nerve points in my back. In an instant the pain disappears. I feel like I've been reborn.

"Are you all right?" Cho asks as I sway on my wobbly legs.

"I am now," I gasp. I hold a hand to my thumping heart. "But remind me never to volunteer to help the Grandmaster show a new move again!"

Chapter 2
Digging

I drive my spade into the muddy ditch then heave a mound of earth onto the steep bank above me. I try to ignore the aches and pains in my body. After a month of Death Touch training, every student is battered and bruised. It takes a lot of practice to target the correct points on the *chi* lines and most of the time we get it wrong!

"My back is killing me," moans Jun, a tall thin boy who is working in another ditch. He stands up and stretches and then calls out to the teacher who is watching us work. "Sensei, the rice fields are already dug. What's the point of all these extra ditches and banks?"

Sensei Shima gives him a hard stare. "A ninja must hear what is silent, see what is invisible and bear what is painful," he says. "If you cannot see what you're doing here, then you need to dig a little longer."

The students in the class all look at one another. The purpose of the ditches is still a mystery to us. Sensei Shima normally teaches us combat and battle tactics, but for the last few weeks we've spent most of our time chopping wood, building fences and digging ditches.

"I expect these ditches to be finished by sunset," Sensei Shima tells us. Then he strides off towards his farmhouse and disappears inside.

"I don't believe it!" Renzo yells. He throws down his spade in disgust. "Sensei Shima goes off to drink tea, while we slave away in the dirt!"

Renzo's friend Yoko wipes mud from her face and grumbles. "Last lesson we were tying back tree branches for him," she says. "Before that he made us carry firewood onto the mountain ridges and out into the fields. None of this makes any sense. We're supposed to be ninja, not gardeners!"

"Too right," Renzo agrees. "When are we going to do something worth doing? The Grandmaster's Death Touch lessons are so much more fun."

He closes his fingers to form a 'snakehead' fist. This is the lethal strike that the Grandmaster has just taught us earlier that morning.

"This lesson is worth doing," says Cho, who has already dug half of her ditch. "It keeps us fit and strong so that we can climb walls, jump high and speed-run."

"But I'm already strong," Renzo argues. He flexes the impressive muscles in his arms and then turns to me. "Taka, you dig my trench."

"Why me?" I protest.

"Because your puny body needs the exercise," he laughs.

Renzo is my rival and so he always picks on me. But now I have completed my first mission and I'm a black belt, I'm no longer scared of him.

"Sensei Shima says a ninja doesn't have to be strong," I reply. "In fact, the best ninja are lean and quick – not fat and slow."

Renzo leaps into my ditch and squares up to me.

"That's fighting talk," he growls. "You think you're a hero just because you saved the ninja Scrolls, don't you? Well, you're not. I heard your father was killed running away from the Battle of Black Eagle. He was a coward – and that means *you* must be too."

Renzo's insult to my dead father makes me explode with anger. I raise my spade to knock him over. In the blink of an eye, Renzo makes his snakehead fist and strikes a nerve point in my shoulder. My arm goes limp and I drop my spade.

"Too weak to hold the spade, are we?" Renzo smirks.

No matter how hard I try, I can't move my arm. It's gone totally numb and hangs limp by my side.

"Unlock my arm!" I demand.

Renzo shrugs in a fake apology. "Sorry, but I haven't learned how to release it yet."

"Then I'll do it," says Cho. She jumps into the ditch and inspects my arm.

"Poor Taka," Renzo mocks. "He needs a girl to rescue him."

"Go and bash your head against a temple bell," Cho snaps, as she tries to find the correct point to release my arm. But after three attempts it stays locked.

"I don't know what Renzo's done to you," she sighs. "You'll have to visit the Grandmaster."

With Cho's help, I climb out of the ditch. The Grandmaster's temple is high on the ridge to the north of us and I head towards the long path that winds up the mountain. I glare at Renzo as I leave.

"You'd better hurry," Renzo laughs. He points to the sun, which is sinking low in the sky. "You still have your ditch to finish."

Chapter 3
Autumn Leaves

"Renzo has certainly mastered *that* skill," the Grandmaster says. He seems both impressed at his student's skill and disappointed with the fact he has used it on me. "But he has yet to master himself," he tells me.

"I know," I reply, as I flex my arm and shake the stiffness from it. "Renzo always wants to prove he's better than me."

"Then that's *his* problem," the Grandmaster says. "It's more important to be the best that *you* can be than to worry about being better than someone else."

He lays a kind hand on my arm.

"Next time, try not to let your anger control you," he advises me. "Anger is like a hot coal. When you grasp it to throw it at someone else, it burns you instead."

He picks up his staff and leaves me in the garden to think about his words of wisdom.

I head back down through the forest. Now it's autumn, all the leaves are turning gold, orange and red. Through a gap in the trees, I spy our village far below. It is hidden deep in a remote valley and can only be reached by a few steep mountain passes. The route is our clan's best-kept secret.

at a pile of fallen leaves as I wander path. Despite the Grandmaster's advice, I'm still furious at what Renzo said about my father. I know so little about him. He was killed by the samurai Lord Oda when I was only a baby.

Was he really a coward?

Further along the path I'm surprised to spot my mother. Then I see she's cutting a puffball mushroom from the base of a tree. Everyone in the village visits her for her powerful herbal medicines. I know that she uses mushroom spores to cure infected wounds.

She looks up in joy. "Taka! What are you doing up here?"

"I had to see the Grandmaster," I explain.

My mother smiles proudly. I realise she has a secret hope that he's preparing me to be the next Grandmaster. I decide not to tell her the real reason for my visit. But I do have to ask one very important question.

"Mother," I say. "Did my father die *running away* from the Battle of Black Eagle?"

Her smile vanishes and she looks shocked. "Who told you that?"

"Renzo," I admit.

My mother scowls. "That boy is a pest. Listen, Taka. Your father was a true warrior."

"But *who* was he? You never talk about him."

My mother sighs. "It's difficult to explain. You see – "

All of a sudden she stops talking. Behind us we hear footsteps crunch through the forest. We glance at each other, worried.

No ninja would make *that* much noise.

Chapter 4
Fatal Message

I disappear into a bush beside the path. My mother hides behind a tree.

Even though we're close to our own village, a ninja must always be on guard. Our clan leader Tenshin has warned us about an increase in samurai patrols. Lord Oda has vowed to destroy every ninja clan in his domain. Four months ago, I stole back our clan's Scrolls from him. He's been hunting the mountains for us ever since.

The crunch of leaves gets closer. The footsteps are heavy and uneven. I can now hear breathing, harsh and rapid.

If the intruder is a samurai, we have to kill him. We can't let him escape to tell Lord Oda where our village is.

My mother pulls out her knife.

I reach into my belt and select three *shuriken*. These are ninja stars. Fast, silent and tipped with deadly poison, they're my weapon of choice.

The bushes ahead begin to rustle. I get ready to throw my *shuriken*.

A man staggers onto the forest path. He's dressed in robes the colour of saffron. He carries a trumpet made from a conch shell and leans on a wooden staff. He appears to be a *yamabushi*, a mountain monk.

The monk falls against a tree and I spot two arrows sticking out of his back.

"Riku!" my mother cries. She darts out from her hiding place.

I look again. He's in disguise, but now I recognise the man's face. He's one of Tenshin's best spies.

Riku collapses into my mother's arms. She lowers him to the ground, opens her medicine bag and starts to tend the arrow wounds.

"No, Akemi ..." Riku groans. "You must ... listen first ..."

Riku's breathing is shallow and his voice is weak. We both lean closer to hear his words.

"I was spying in Black Eagle Castle ... I heard Lord Oda ... I don't know how ... but he's found out where our village is!"

My mother and I look at one another in shock.

"Then we must close the mountain passes," my mother says.

"Too late," says Riku, as he gasps his last dying breath. "Lord Oda ... is on the march ... with his army. They'll be here by sunrise."

Chapter 5
Invisible Defences

I join Cho in the village square just before dawn. Like me, she's wearing her black *gi*, the ninja uniform. It has our emblem of two hawks on the front.

We take our place among the rest of the clan. Every ninja is dressed for battle and carries a weapon. Cho is armed with her double-edged sword. Jun has a pair of *kama* – curved blades with wooden shafts. Renzo twirls his *nunchaku* – two sticks joined by a chain. Of course, he is showing off to Yoko who is wearing her *shuko* – cat claws. My belt is packed with *shuriken*.

Renzo glances over at me. "Didn't expect to see that coward here!" he says to Yoko.

I feel my anger rise.

Cho grabs my arm to stop me. "He's not your enemy today!" she tells me. "Lord Oda is."

I try to control my temper. "I know," I say. "But we should all be on the same side!"

Our clan leader, Tenshin, climbs the village watch tower with Sensei Shima. He holds up his hand to get us to listen.

"All ninja know that the greatest victory is the battle not fought," he declares. "But in this case, Lord Oda has left us with no choice. We *must* defend our homes. But do not fear, for

Sensei Shima and I have been planning for just such an attack."

He nods at Sensei Shima, who orders two men to divert the stream that runs through our village. They open a floodgate and the ditches we dug fill up in minutes. I gasp with surprise as a large ring of water surrounds us. Cho and the other ninja students stare in equal amazement. Sensei Shima has built a moat around the village.

His words come back to me. 'A ninja must ... see what is invisible.'

At last I can see all the defences that we've been working on this past month:

- The high banks of earth we built are really a maze of walls to protect us from an enemy army.

- The paths between the paddy fields are so narrow only one person at a time can pass along them.

- The bamboo fences we made form a spiked barrier around the village square.

- The tree branches that we tied back at the edge of the forest are booby traps. The trip-wires are hidden in the bushes.

We didn't realise at the time, but we were turning the village into a fortress!

On the ridge to the east, a spiral of smoke rises into the dawn sky. It's a warning signal from one of our ninja scouts.

"Lord Oda is here!" Tenshin announces. His face is grave. "Let us welcome him and his army in true ninja style."

Then he grins and raises his famous and lethal Sword of Destruction. The edge of the blade is jagged like a saw.

The clan all raise their weapons in salute and we shout a mighty battle cry.

The roar of our voices makes me feel strong and brave.

Then we fall silent as a gold flag with the crest of a black eagle appears on the ridge. Then another. And another ...

Soon the whole mountain ridge is lined with flags. They flap in the wind like a flock of vultures.

In spite of the bravery I felt during the battle cry, the sight of so many warriors sends an icy cold shiver down my spine.

Lord Oda has brought an army of over a thousand samurai.

Against a village of less than a hundred ninja.

What chance do we have?

Chapter 6
Ten to One

"Lord Oda demands your surrender," the samurai messenger states. Having ridden his horse down the valley, he waits at the border of our village for our reply.

Tenshin laughs at the idea, then shouts back. "Tell Lord Oda that we demand *his* surrender."

The samurai is stunned by Tenshin's answer. "B ... but there are ten of us to every one of you!"

"Yes," Tenshin agrees cheerfully. "It's a shame you didn't bring more men. Your defeat will be swift and shameful."

The samurai is unable to believe his ears. He pulls on his horse's reins and gallops back up the valley to tell Lord Oda.

I am shocked too. "Does Tenshin really think we can win?" I whisper to Cho.

"Think?" answers the Grandmaster, who appears behind me. "He *knows* we can."

"But their army is sure to beat us," Cho says. Her eyes scan the rows upon rows of swords, spears and battle-axes.

The Grandmaster leans on his staff and taps a finger to his head. "A winner wins in his

mind first, then goes to war. A loser goes to war and then seeks to win. Tenshin has already won the battle in his head. That's what you both need to do now."

I follow the Grandmaster's advice and try to imagine our victory, but the thought of the bloody conflict terrifies me.

The Grandmaster lays a hand on my arm and studies me with his blind eyes. "Are you scared, Taka?"

I realise there's no point in lying to the Grandmaster. He may be blind, but he always sees the truth. I hope Renzo can't hear my reply as I admit, "Yes."

"Good. You should be," says the Grandmaster, to my surprise. "Fear can make a mouse attack a lion. Use your fear to give you strength. Remember the skills I've taught you and you will live to see another day."

With that, he hobbles away to offer a boost to the other young ninja who face their first battle.

"Don't worry," says Cho. "I'll protect your back."

I offer a smile in return. "And I'll protect yours."

As we bump fists in a bond of friendship, an angry cry echoes through the valley. I look up and see that the samurai messenger has delivered our clan leader's reply to Lord Oda.

Lord Oda roars down at us from high on the ridge. "PREPARE TO DIE, NINJA!"

Chapter 7
Traps and Trenches

Lord Oda and his army thunder down the mountain like a tidal wave.

I grab my *shuriken*, but fear fills my heart and my hand begins to tremble. Then I look at Cho and remember the Grandmaster's words. I feel a surge of strength.

I am a ninja and I'll protect my family, friends and clan with my life if I have to.

As the first line of samurai advance into the trees, their horses' hooves trigger the hidden trip-wires. Long branches whip back and knock the samurai from their saddles. The charge turns into chaos as the horses run off in different directions without their riders.

But a second wave of samurai are not far behind. There are no tree traps left now, so they reach the valley bottom unharmed. Tenshin orders a group of ninja to let loose a volley of flaming arrows from their bows.

The arrows shoot through the air ... but miss every single samurai!

I groan in despair before I realise that the samurai weren't the target – the wood piles we stacked in the fields are. The piles are soaked in lamp oil and gunpowder and explode into lethal firebombs that engulf the enemy in flames.

Our clan lets out a huge cheer as the samurai advance is stopped in its tracks.

"We're going to win this battle!" I shout, and I punch the air in victory.

"It's not over yet," Cho warns.

She points to where Lord Oda is rallying his forces to launch a fresh assault. A new troop of samurai avoids the flaming wood piles and charges down the only road into our village. The route has been left open to attack and I fear our defences have failed.

But then the whole troop disappears.

We hear their moans and cries of pain. The troop ran straight into a deep trench covered with a mesh of sticks and autumn leaves. The trench is filled with sharp stones and bamboo spikes. The samurai had no idea it was there until they hit the bottom!

Lord Oda goes into a rage when he realises he has lost over a third of his men already. "I'LL MAKE YOU SUFFER FOR YOUR NINJA TRICKS!" he screams.

Lord Oda directs what is left of his army to head to the south. He leads the charge across the moat himself. The deep water slows their horses and the ninja with bows shoot arrow after arrow, picking off as many samurai as they can.

But the moat can't stop an entire army. Soon the samurai are clambering onto the banks and storming the village.

The battle between ninja and samurai now truly begins.

Chapter 8
Coward

"ATTACK!" Tenshin shouts as he rushes forward to engage with the enemy. His Sword of Destruction cuts through the ranks of samurai like they were origami soldiers.

Sensei Shima is right behind Tenshin. His sword is a blur as he and the other clan members fight to defend our village.

Renzo is the first of the young ninja to do battle. His spinning *nunchaku* knock out samurai after samurai. As much as I dislike Renzo, I have to admire his bravery. The rest of the ninja are inspired by his courage. They raise their weapons and charge forward.

I stand back-to-back with Cho as Lord Oda's army surges across the rice fields and into the village. Cho's double-edged sword means she's always on the attack, no matter which way she swings her weapon.

A samurai leaps at me and Cho stops him dead before he gets anywhere near.

"Thanks!" I gasp. "I owe you one."

Two samurai rush at Cho. I double-throw two *shuriken*. The ninja stars hit both samurai in the throat.

"Now I owe you," Cho says as her two attackers fall to the ground, with blood pouring from their wounds.

Then I spot a samurai with a barbed spear rush at the Grandmaster.

"Watch out!" I cry, even though I know the Grandmaster can't see him.

But the Grandmaster is already aware of the danger. He flicks the end of his staff towards the charging samurai. The hollow end of the staff sends a poison dart into the man's neck. The samurai drops to the ground, dead.

Another samurai slices downwards with his sword. The Grandmaster hits him in the shoulder with his staff. As the samurai drops his weapon, the Grandmaster strikes with a snakehead fist just below the man's heart. The samurai collapses – a victim of the Death Touch.

More samurai attack the blind Grandmaster. Each suffer a similar fate. Soon there's a pile of bodies knee-deep around him.

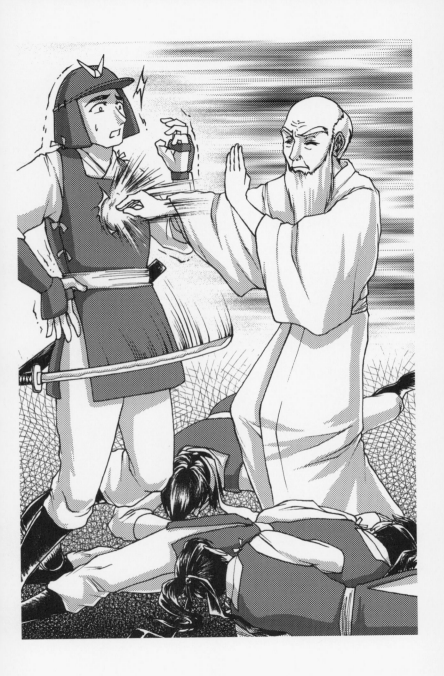

I realise the Grandmaster can look after himself and concentrate on fighting my own battles. The village is now swarming with samurai and our clan is in danger of being overcome.

I throw *shuriken* after *shuriken*, and take down as many of the enemy as I can. But then I reach into my belt and discover I've only got one ninja star left. And there are still hundreds of samurai ...

I hear a cry for help. To my right, a samurai with a huge battle-axe cuts through the chain of Renzo's *nunchaku* and kicks him to the ground. Renzo has no way to defend himself. He is about to be chopped in half.

Without a second thought, I throw my last *shuriken* to save my rival. The ninja star strikes the samurai in the arm and he loses grip on his axe. But the poison is slow to act and the samurai draws his sword to kill Renzo.

I rush forward and launch myself into a flying kick. My foot smashes into the samurai's chest. He staggers backwards, trips over a body and ends up skewered on the spiked bamboo fence.

Renzo stares up at me in shock.

"No need to thank me," I say, as I hurry off to find Cho again.

But Renzo leaps to his feet and calls after me. "I was wrong," he shouts. "You're no coward."

Then he looks past me and narrows his eyes in fury. "But Cho is."

As I turn, I see my friend flee the battle and escape up the mountain.

Chapter 9
Death Touch

I can't believe Cho would run away. We'd sworn to protect each other. But when I look around the village, I realise our defeat is inevitable.

The sheer size of Lord Oda's army is too great. Half of my clan are already dead or dying.

Tenshin calls for any ninja still alive to retreat to the village square.

I run with Renzo for this last stronghold. A samurai is right behind us, slashing with his sword. We turn into an alley and leap over a hidden ditch. The samurai follows but he doesn't see the ditch. We hear his screams as he tumbles into the trap.

Renzo and I are the last ninja to make it into the village square. Tenshin and Sensei Shima rush to close the gate in the spiked fence.

I spot my mother among the survivors and breathe a sigh of relief. We are safe … but only for the moment.

Lord Oda and his army surround us on all sides. The samurai begin to burn our farmhouses to the ground. I even see a fire blazing in the Grandmaster's temple high on the ridge. Lord Oda is destroying everything.

"You should have surrendered while you had the chance," Lord Oda yells to us. "Now you will all die."

He orders his men to attack. They chop at the spiked bamboo fence with their axes. Tenshin and the other ninja do their best to fend them off. But the samurai are unstoppable. They break through into the square.

Sensei Shima is cut down in an instant. Jun is swamped by five samurai at once and doesn't get up again. Yoko fights as fiercely as a tiger but is soon wounded. Renzo snatches up a broken spear and races to her defence.

I have no more *shuriken*. When a samurai charges at me, I can only fling mud into his eyes. As soon as he is blinded, I front-kick him in the gut and knock him out with a hammerfist strike to the top of the head.

Then I see the Grandmaster, battling three samurai on his own with his staff snapped in

half. As I fight my way to him, I come face-to-face with Lord Oda.

He glares at me.

"I recognise your eyes, ninja!" he snarls. "You're the one who stole back the Scrolls."

"And I recognise your ugly red scar!" I reply in insult.

I look to my left and spy someone's sword on the ground. If I can kill Lord Oda, then the battle would be over – like cutting the head off a snake!

Lord Oda sees me glance at the weapon and grins. "Do you think you can get to it in time?" he taunts.

I realise this is my chance to avenge my murdered father. I dive for the sword. Lord Oda lunges to cut me in half ... but my move was a fake.

As Lord Oda attacks the wrong way, he exposes his chest. I switch direction, dart forwards and strike him with a snakehead fist in the heart.

Death Touch!

But Lord Oda doesn't die. He just laughs at me.

Chapter 10
A Price to Pay

"Your ninja magic won't work on me!" Lord Oda says.

I stare in shock at the samurai lord. I know that I hit the exact nerve point the Grandmaster taught me. There is no way Lord Oda should have survived my attack. Was he immortal? Or had I got the Death Touch wrong?

Lord Oda sees the painful confusion in my face.

"I was born to survive," he reveals with a grin. "My heart is on the *opposite* side."

He taps the right side of his chest. Now I understand why the Death Touch didn't work – the strike points are reversed.

"I told you I'd have my revenge," Lord Oda gloats and he thrusts with his sword.

"NO! Not my son!" my mother cries. She leaps to save me.

My mother lands between us and Lord Oda's sword goes straight through her instead of me.

"Mother!" I cry as she collapses in my arms, blood pouring from her stomach. I clasp her to me to try to stop the bleeding. "Please don't die," I beg.

"Taka ... don't cry," she groans. "Sometimes ... a price must be paid ... to protect those you love ..."

Her eyes close and her body goes limp in my arms.

"*NO!*" I scream.

Lord Oda stands over me, staring at my mother's dead body.

Through my tears of grief, I look to the sky and see dark red autumn leaves fall like drops of blood into the valley.

Then I see a river of black flowing down the mountain. I have to wipe away my tears before I realise that it's another ninja clan. Cho is leading them. I can see her double-edged sword glinting in the morning sun.

A samurai officer rushes over to Lord Oda.

"We must retreat, Lord Oda!" he insists, with a fearful glance at the new ninja clan.

But Lord Oda doesn't move. His bodyguards have to drag him away as the ninja clan storm into the village and begin to wipe out his army. The rest of the samurai drop their weapons and flee for their lives.

As the last of them disappear over the ridge, a huge cheer of victory fills the valley.

Against all the odds, the ninja have won.

Chapter 11
Deadly Mission

I pack my belt with as many *shuriken* as I can find. Then I fill another bag with rope, *shuko* climbing claws, a knife, my mother's herbal medicine, a flint and steel for making fire, food, a water skin and spare clothes.

Before I head out the door, I take one last look around the wreck of my house. My bed is ripped to shreds. The kitchen is smashed to pieces. And the hearth is cold and empty where a fire always used to burn. Now my mother is dead, the place no longer feels like home.

There's a knock at the door. It's Cho – the star of the battle. She had the good sense to light the distress beacon in the Grandmaster's temple and summon the nearest ninja clan to our aid.

"Are you ready to go?" Cho asks me.

We may have won the battle, but Tenshin has decided that the clan must move deeper into the mountains and find a new hidden valley.

"I'm not going with the clan," I reply.

Cho's eyes widen in surprise.

"I have to find Lord Oda."

"*What?*" she cries.

"If someone doesn't stop him, he'll only return with a bigger army, hunt us down and destroy our clan forever," I explain. "I plan to cut the head off the snake."

Cho looks at me as if I'm mad. "Have you told the Grandmaster about this?"

I shake my head.

"But a mission like that is a death wish," she argues. "With all the bodyguards he has, you'll never get close enough to him."

"I've been close twice before," I reply. "I can do it again."

"Not on your own," she says. "I'll come with you."

"No," I say, although I'm touched by her loyalty. "It's too great a risk."

Cho gives me a hard stare. "We made a battle bond," she reminds me. "*You protect my back, I protect yours.* As this battle isn't over, our bond isn't either."

I smile at her. "You're a true friend," I say. I realise my chances of success are far greater with Cho by my side.

Just as we're about to leave, Renzo appears. "I overheard your plan. I want to come too."

"Why?" I ask. I am suspicious of his reasons.

Renzo bows his head in remorse. "I owe you my life," he explains. "As a ninja brother, it's my duty to help you any way I can."

I turn to Cho for her opinion. She just shrugs. "He could carry all our bags."

Although Renzo is my rival, I respect his strength and courage. "You realise there may be no going back?" I say.

Renzo grins. "I like a challenge!"

The decision made, we all bump fists in a battle bond. Then we slip silently into the night.

Three ninja on a deadly mission ...

Our books are tested
for children and young people by
children and young people.

Thanks to everyone who consulted on
a manuscript for their time and effort in
helping us to make our books better
for our readers.

Have you read...

Ninja: First Mission

He waits under the floor-boards. He's been hidden for over an hour, lying still as a stone. His name is Taka. This is his first mission as a ninja and he must not fail...

When the Grandmaster sends Taka on a special mission, this is his last chance to prove himself.

But the mission is dangerous. To fail is to die, and Taka has failed before...

OUT NOW!

Coming 2014...

Ninja: Assassin

With his ninja clan on the run and his mother dead, Taka vows to find Lord Oda and bring him to justice.

But Taka's training is not yet complete. Can he fulfill his destiny as an assassin?

Or will a dark secret prevent him from completing his deadly mission?

www.barringtonstoke.co.uk